SHIRLEY HUGHES
UP AND UP

THE BODLEY HEAD

LONDON

0-370-30179-X
Copyright © Shirley Hughes 1979
First published in 1979 by
The Bodley Head Children's Books
an imprint of The Random Century Group Ltd
20 Vauxhall Bridge Road, London SW1V 2SA
Printed in Hong Kong
Reprinted 1982, 1985, 1991

FOR ED AND TOM

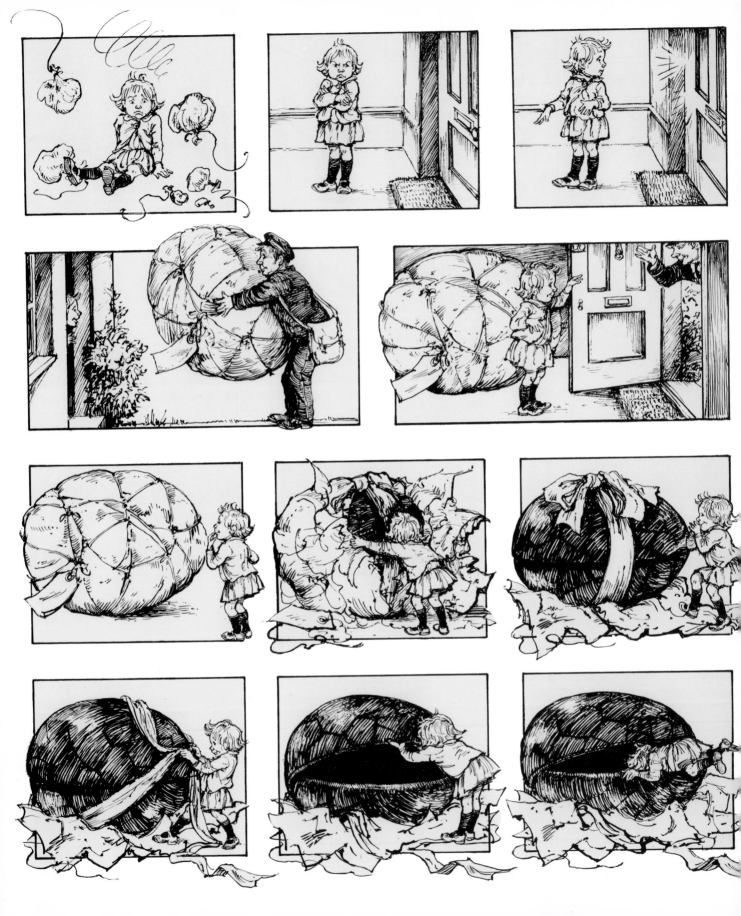

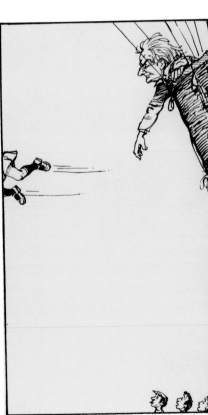